Step into
NARNIA
A Journey Through
THE LION, THE WITCH AND THE WARDROBE

ISBN: 0-00-720611-9

First published in the United States of America in 2005 by HarperCollins Children's Books,
a division of HarperCollins Publishers, 1350 Avenue of the Americas, New York, NY10019.

This edition published in Great Britain in 2005 by HarperCollins Children's Books,
an imprint of HarperCollins Publishers, 77-85 Fulham Palace Road, Hammersmith, London W6 8JB.
Visit the HarperCollins Children's Books website at www.harpercollinschildrensbooks.co.uk

www.narnia.com

1 3 5 7 9 10 8 6 4 2

A Journey Through

THE LION, THE WITCH AND THE WARDROBE

by E. J. Kirk

Based on the classic book by C. S. Lewis

HarperCollins *Children's Books*

WHAT'S INSIDE

CAVES TO CASTLES

BATTLES

POWERFUL MAGIC

THE MOVIE

THIS SIDE OF THE WARDROBE

Our adventure begins when four curious children explore a huge, old house. One of them, named Lucy, discovers a secret passageway that leads to the magical world of Narnia. Soon she and her siblings are all there, helping new friends fight a battle against evil!

Lucy, Edmund, Susan and Peter live in London when World War II begins. The Germans are dropping bombs on their city.

The Professor's house is huge and has many winding hallways and empty rooms. One rainy day, the children go exploring.

For safety, the children are sent to live with the Professor in a big house in the country.

In a spare room, they find a big wardrobe. Lucy discovers it is a magic doorway to another world.

Next moment Lucy found that what was rubbing against her face and hands was no longer soft fur but something hard and rough and even prickly. "Why, it is just like branches of trees!" exclaimed Lucy.

Lucy is the first to pass through the wardrobe into Narnia. She suddenly finds herself in a snowy forest, where she discovers a lamppost!

THE WHITE WITCH'S WINTER

In Narnia, the children discover a frozen world under the spell of the evil White Witch, who calls herself the Queen of Narnia. They meet both good and evil creatures.

Lucy meets a strange but friendly creature named Mr. Tumnus, who invites her to his home. They have tea, and he warns her about the White Witch. When Lucy travels back through the wardrobe, her brothers and sister don't believe her tale of Narnia.

Edmund goes through the wardrobe next. In Narnia, he meets the evil Witch, who invites him into her sledge and feeds him enchanted Turkish Delight. The candy makes him want to do whatever the Witch tells him—and to crave more candy!

Edmund keeps his meeting with the Witch a secret. Soon, all four children travel through the wardrobe to Narnia. In the frozen forest, Mr. and Mrs. Beaver welcome them into their home. The children learn about the Great Lion, Aslan.

Edmund sneaks out of the Beavers' home to find the Witch's castle. The Witch's home is filled with her evil minions and with good creatures that have been turned into stone.

"Always winter and never Christmas; think of that!"

THE AGE OF ASLAN

Narnia's legends say the White Witch's evil time will end only when four human children are crowned kings and queens and sit on the four thrones at Cair Paravel. When Aslan arrives, spring comes to Narnia and the White Witch's magic weakens. After bloody battles are fought and magic spells are cast, the legend is fulfilled.

Lucy, Susan, Peter and the Beavers meet Father Christmas, who gives the children magical gifts.

At Cair Paravel, Aslan crowns Peter, Susan, Edmund and Lucy as kings and queens of Narnia, and they sit on the four thrones just as the legends foretold. The Witch's evil time in Narnia is over!

Aslan and his friends gather on a hilltop that has a beautiful yellow silk tent and a mysterious Stone Table. Here, Peter fights his first battle. Later, following the Deep Magic practice, the White Witch kills Aslan in Edmund's place, and Aslan uses the Deeper Magic to return to life.

With Peter leading Aslan's forces, the White Witch is defeated in a big battle at the Fords of Beruna. Edmund is badly injured, but Lucy uses her magic cordial to cure him.

"Once a king or queen in Narnia, always a king or queen."

Lucy

about me

Nickname: Lu

Narnia name: Queen Lucy the Valiant

Year born: 1932

Family order: Youngest

Personality: Usually cheerful, always truthful, always brave

Favorite thing: Making friends

Known for: Discovering Narnia

Best friend in Narnia: Mr. Tumnus, the Faun

Most exciting moment: Riding on Aslan's back

Heroic moment: Tending to the wounded after the final battle against the Witch

Gifts from Father Christmas

Cordial bottle

Made of diamond, not glass; contains the juice of the fire-flowers that grow in the mountains of the sun. Used for healing wounds and making sick people healthy

Small dagger

To defend herself when she is in trouble

Dear Diary,

Today I discovered a magical world! I stepped into the wardrobe at the Professor's house and ended up in a very strange place called Narnia.

I met a Faun, had tea in his lovely cave and listened to him play the flute. (That put me to sleep.) Then he told me about the evil White Witch.

Narnia was exciting and scary and wonderful, all at the same time! I was there for many hours, but when I came back it was as though no time had passed at all. Susan, Peter and Edmund thought I made up the whole story. That makes me so cross!

I so want them to believe me—and I want all of us to explore Narnia together.

Love,
Lucy

Edmund

Nickname: Ed
Narnia name: King Edmund the Just
Year born: 1930
Personality: At first, grumpy, jealous and dishonest; later, brave and fair
Favorite thing: Turkish Delight
Scariest moment: When the Witch and her henchmen almost kill him
Heroic moment: Breaking the Witch's wand in the Great Battle (a very good thing)

In Secret

After Edmund is rescued, he and Aslan have a private conversation. No one hears what they say—but it changes Edmund forever. Afterward, Edmund apologizes to Peter, Susan and Lucy, and all is forgiven. How would you feel if you were Edmund?

Gifts from Father Christmas

None. Edmund didn't meet Father Christmas because he had gone off to find the Witch (and, he hoped, more Turkish Delight).

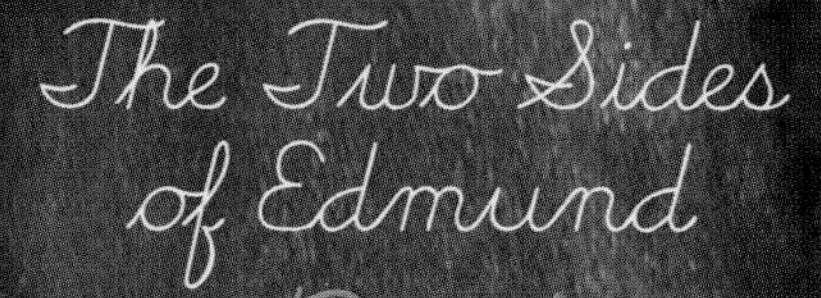

Bad

Tends toward bad temper, especially when tired or sad

Displays bad manners while eating Turkish Delight

Lies to others when he denies having been to Narnia

Good

Apologizes to Lucy for not believing her when she first went to Narnia

Fights bravely in the battle against the White Witch

Realizes that the Witch's wand must be destroyed—and smashes it

Susan

Nickname: Su

Narnia name:
Queen Susan the Gentle

Year born: 1928

Personality:
Mothering, sensible, kind

Known for:
Being the greatest archer in Narnia

Heroic moment:
Suggesting she and Lucy go with Aslan to meet the White Witch

Can You Hear Me?

Susan blows the horn Father Christmas gave her—and Peter hears her call, even though he's far away. Help find the right path from Susan's horn to Peter's sword.

(ANSWER ON LAST PAGE)

B

A

C

Gifts from Father Christmas

Bow and quiver of arrows

To be used only in great need

Horn

Susan blows it and help magically arrives.

PETER

KING PETER THE MAGNIFICENT

FACTS

NICKNAME: NONE. EVERYONE CALLS HIM PETER.

NARNIA NAMES: KING PETER THE MAGNIFICENT, HIGH KING PETER, SIR PETER WOLF'S-BANE

YEAR BORN: 1927

FAMILY ORDER: OLDEST

PERSONALITY: BRAVE, STRONG, LOYAL

HOBBY: EXPLORING OUTDOORS

LOOKS UP TO: ASLAN

KNOWN FOR: CALMNESS IN THE HEAT OF A BATTLE

SCARIEST MOMENT: BATTLING THE WITCH FACE-TO-FACE

HEROIC MOMENT: SAVING SUSAN BY DEFEATING MAUGRIM

BATTLE PLANS

AFTER DISCUSSING THE TWO BATTLE PLANS WITH ASLAN, PETER CHOOSES TO CUT OFF THE WITCH BEFORE SHE REACHES HER CASTLE.

OTHER FAMOUS LEADERS

PETER IS A FIERCE FIGHTER AND GREAT LEADER ON THE BATTLEFIELD. SO WERE THESE LEADERS. MATCH THE LEADER WITH THE COUNTRY.

(ANSWERS ON LAST PAGE)

1. ALEXANDER THE GREAT	A. MONGOLIA
2. JULIUS CAESAR	B. THE ROMAN EMPIRE
3. GENGHIS KHAN	C. MACEDONIA
4. HENRY V	D. UNITED STATES
5. JOAN OF ARC	E. ENGLAND
6. GEORGE WASHINGTON	F. FRANCE

GIFTS FROM FATHER CHRISTMAS

A SHIELD AND A SWORD THE SWORD HAS A SHEATH AND A SWORD BELT AND IS JUST THE RIGHT SIZE FOR PETER TO USE.

...AND WHEN HE SHAKES HIS MANE,
WE SHALL HAVE SPRING AGAIN.

Riding

What's the most **wonderful**, heart-thumpingly exciting, **magical ride** you have ever had? Was it **galloping along** on the back of a great big horse? Or **riding** a bike for the first time? Or **jumping** off a diving board? Now imagine that you are riding a larger-than-life, warm and furry animal—and not just any animal but a lion,

THE GREAT LION.

You're riding on Aslan's back, just like Susan and Lucy!

WHAT FOLKS SAY ABOUT ASLAN

"ASLAN A MAN! CERTAINLY NOT. I TELL YOU HE IS THE KING OF THE WOOD AND THE SON OF THE GREAT EMPEROR-BEYOND-THE-SEA. DON'T YOU KNOW WHO IS THE KING OF BEASTS? ASLAN IS A LION—*THE* LION, THE GREAT LION."
—MR. BEAVER

"YOUR WINTER HAS BEEN DESTROYED, I TELL YOU! THIS IS ASLAN'S DOING."
—THE WHITE WITCH'S DWARF DRIVER

the Lion

ASLAN'S MOST MAGICAL MOMENT

"And now to business. I feel I am going

Wrong will be right,
when Aslan comes in sight,
At the sound of his roar,
sorrows will be no more,
When he bears his teeth,
winter meets its death...

HOW BIG IS ASLAN?

Compare your hand to the size of his. Even though your hand is small, the footprints of the mice at the right are even smaller than yours. Yet the tiny mice were able to free Aslan by gnawing through the ropes that bound him. Can you think of some other times when someone smaller was able to help in a big way?

(Answers on last page)

to roar. You had better put your fingers in your ears." —ASLAN

FRIENDS AND HELPERS

Peter, Susan, Edmund and Lucy come across many kind creatures in Narnia. Here's how five of their best helpers stack up.

REPORT CARD

Mr. Beaver

Hospitality: A* Takes Peter fishing with him

Fishing: A++

Dam building: A+

Effort: A* Works hard at all he does

Bravery: A

Narnia history: A

Planning: A+* Locks dam door to delay the Witch

Insight: A* Knows Edmund had met the Witch

Comments:

Mr. Beaver meets the children in the woods, welcomes them into his home and later guides them through Narnia. He is a great helper and very kind!

REPORT CARD

Mrs. Beaver

Sewing: A+

Cooking: A* Makes a fine sticky marmalade roll

Housekeeping: B+* Neat, but a bit of a pack rat

Hospitality: A+

Bravery: A

Packing: B* Makes good choices, but could be quicker

Planning: A+* Calculates how long it will take the Witch to reach them

Comments:

Mrs. Beaver keeps the children well fed as they travel through Narnia. She and Mr. Beaver make the children feel welcome and safe.

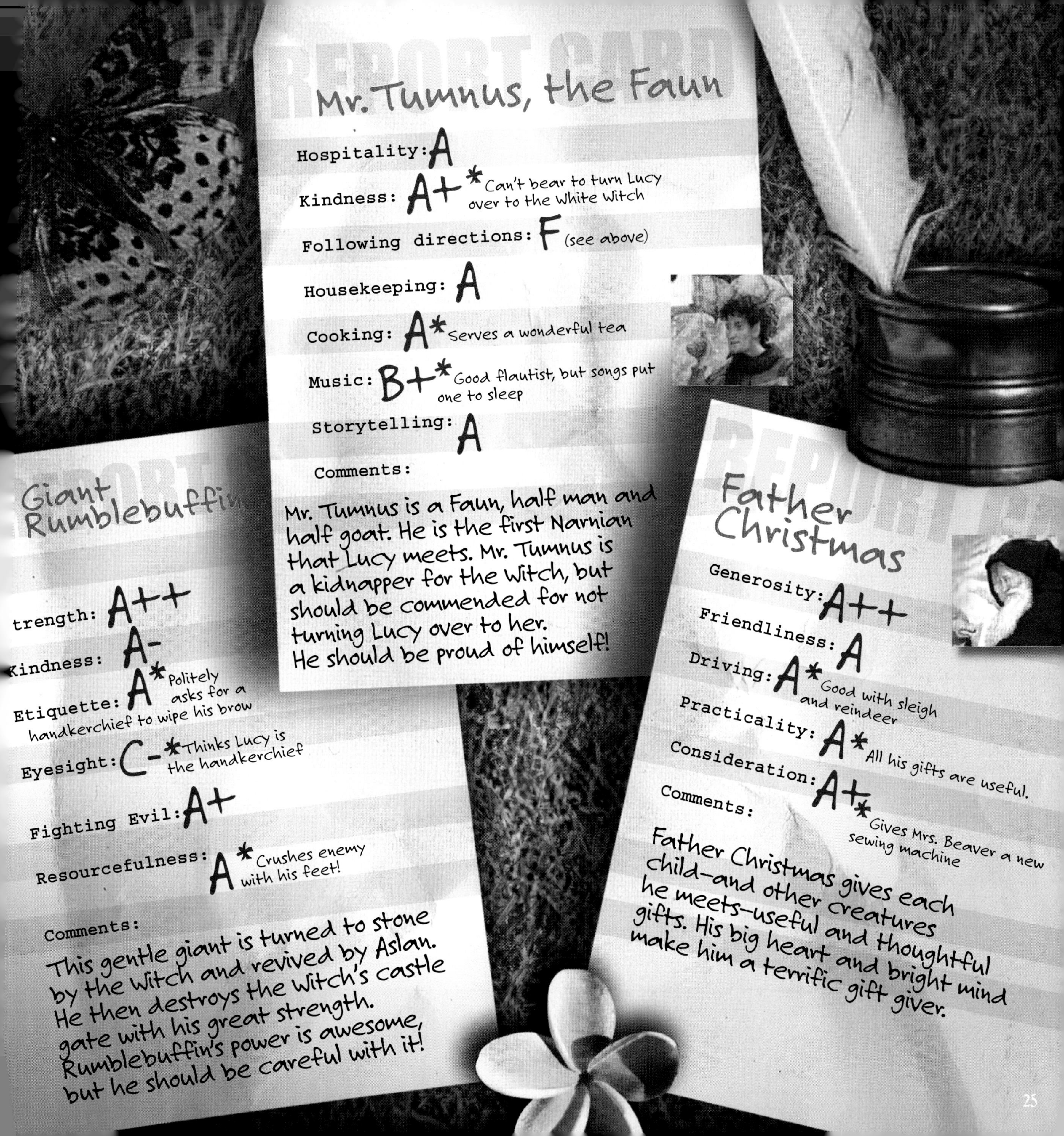

REPORT CARD

Mr. Tumnus, the Faun

Hospitality: A

Kindness: A+ * Can't bear to turn Lucy over to the White Witch

Following directions: F (see above)

Housekeeping: A

Cooking: A* Serves a wonderful tea

Music: B+* Good flautist, but songs put one to sleep

Storytelling: A

Comments:

Mr. Tumnus is a Faun, half man and half goat. He is the first Narnian that Lucy meets. Mr. Tumnus is a kidnapper for the Witch, but should be commended for not turning Lucy over to her. He should be proud of himself!

REPORT CARD

Giant Rumblebuffin

trength: A++

Kindness: A-

Etiquette: A* Politely asks for a handkerchief to wipe his brow

Eyesight: C-* Thinks Lucy is the handkerchief

Fighting Evil: A+

Resourcefulness: A* Crushes enemy with his feet!

Comments:

This gentle giant is turned to stone by the Witch and revived by Aslan. He then destroys the Witch's castle gate with his great strength. Rumblebuffin's power is awesome, but he should be careful with it!

REPORT CARD

Father Christmas

Generosity: A++

Friendliness: A

Driving: A* Good with sleigh and reindeer

Practicality: A* All his gifts are useful.

Consideration: A+* Gives Mrs. Beaver a new sewing machine

Comments:

Father Christmas gives each child—and other creatures he meets—useful and thoughtful gifts. His big heart and bright mind make him a terrific gift giver.

WANTED
WHITE WITCH
ALIAS: Jadis, Queen of Charn, Empress of the Lone Islands and—she says—Queen of Narnia
APPEARANCE: Looks human— but don't be fooled!
TRAVELS WITH: Dwarf
GETAWAY VEHICLE: A sledge pulled by two white reindeer
LAST SEEN WEARING: White fur up to her throat, gold crown. Carries a magic wand.
DISTINCTIVE FEATURE: BRIGHT RED MOUTH
BEWARE:
ARMED AND DANGEROUS

"She is a perfectly terrible person!

She calls herself the Queen of Narnia though she has no right to be queen at all, and all the Fauns and Dryads and Naiads and Dwarfs and Animals—at least all the good ones—simply hate her. And she can turn people into stone and do all kinds of horrible things." —Lucy

". . . bad all through."
—Mrs. Beaver

"THOUGH THE WITCH KNEW THE DEEP MAGIC, THERE IS A MAGIC DEEPER STILL WHICH SHE DID NOT KNOW. HER KNOWLEDGE GOES BACK ONLY TO THE DAWN OF TIME."

—ASLAN

excerpt from: **Witches Quarterly**
10 of My Favorite Things
by Jadis, The White Witch of Narnia

1. Bossing people around.
2. Creating evil food and treats.
3. Tricking Sons of Adam into thinking I'm nice. Ha!
4. Changing people and animals into statues.
5. Getting the best of Aslan.
6. Keeping Narnia cold and wintry forever.
7. Riding upon my sledge.
8. Hearing myself called Queen or Empress.
9. Being evil.
10. Being evil. (It's so good, I thought I'd list it twice.)

EVIL CREATURES

MEET—OR HOPE THAT YOU DON'T!—SOME OF THE WHITE WITCH'S EVIL SERVANTS.

DEAR EDITOR:

WHY DO WOLVES ALWAYS GET A BAD RAP? THAT'S WHAT I WANT TO KNOW. WHEN WAS THE LAST TIME YOU READ A STORY ABOUT A NICE WOLF? CAN'T THINK OF ONE, CAN YOU? BUT LOOK FOR A MEAN WOLF, AND THERE'S NOOOOOOOOO PROBLEM. YOU'VE GOT THE BIG BAD WOLF OF LITTLE RED RIDING HOOD FAME, AND THE GUY THAT BLOWS DOWN THOSE THREE LITTLE PIGS' HOUSES. WOLVES AREN'T ALL BAD. CAN I HELP IT IF THE WITCH WAS THE ONLY ONE WHO WOULD GIVE ME WORK?

SO, ALL YOU CHILDREN OUT THERE: IF YOU EVER WRITE A FAIRY TALE, FIND SOME OTHER ANIMAL TO BE THE BAD GUY. HOW ABOUT A DASTARDLY DEER? OR A MAN-EATING MOUSE? STOP PICKING ON US WOLVES.

SINCERELY,
MAUGRIM

MAUGRIM IS A HUGE GRAY WOLF THAT RUNS THE WITCH'S SECRET POLICE. THEY SNEAK THROUGH NARNIA, ARRESTING INNOCENT CREATURES SO THE WITCH CAN TURN THEM INTO STONE STATUES. MAUGRIM IS SLY; EDMUND THINKS HE IS A STATUE AT FIRST, AND PETER THINKS HE IS A BEAR—BUT NOT FOR LONG!

WANTED
MAUGRIM

TRAVELS WITH: A PACK OF WOLVES

JOB: CHIEF OF THE WITCH'S SECRET POLICE

DESCRIPTION: SHARP TEETH, LARGE BUILD, GRAY FUR

WANTED
THE WITCH'S DWARF

JOB: WITCH'S DRIVER AND MESSENGER

TRAVELS WITH: TWO REINDEER

DESCRIPTION: LONG BEARD, RED HOOD; VERY, VERY SHORT

WHILE THERE ARE GOOD AND BAD DWARFS IN NARNIA, THE WITCH'S DWARF IS BAD WITH A CAPITAL B! AS THE WITCH'S SLEDGE DRIVER, HE CRUELLY WHIPS THE REINDEER AND EDMUND.

HORRIBLE HENCHMEN

THE WHITE WITCH HAS A VARIETY OF WICKED WARRIORS AT HER COMMAND. SHE CALLS THEM ALL TOGETHER FOR HER GREATEST MOMENT: KILLING ASLAN. ON THE FIELDS OF BERUNA THEY BATTLE PETER'S FORCES. SOME OF HER HORRIBLE HENCHMEN ARE FAMILIAR CREATURES, BUT OTHERS ARE NOT—IN FACT, NO ONE REALLY KNOWS WHAT SOME OF THEM ARE. HERE'S A BEST-GUESS BESTIARY OF BAD GUYS.

MINOTAURS:
ENORMOUS MEN WITH BULLS' HEADS

BOGGLES:
SCARY SPIRITS

WEREWOLVES:

PART HUMAN,
PART WOLF—
ALL MEAN

SPECTERS:

CREATURES
TOO HORRIBLE
TO DESCRIBE

OGRES:

MAN-EATING,
GIANT MONSTERS,
WITH HUGE TEETH

CHEERIO!

The Pevensie children live in London, England, until they are sent to the country to stay with Professor Kirke.

London is an old city located along a river called the Thames (pronounced *temz*). It is the capital of the United Kingdom, which includes England, Wales, Scotland and Northern Ireland.

THE UNITED KINGDOM

SCOTLAND

NORTHERN IRELAND

PROFESSOR'S HOUSE

ENGLAND

WALES

LONDON

The flag of the United Kingdom is called the Union Flag or Union Jack. It has three crosses, representing the three kingdoms that are united under one rule:

The cross of St. George (square red cross) stands for England and Wales.

The cross of St. Andrew (diagonal white cross) represents Scotland.

Big Ben

Big Ben is the bell that rings each hour in a 316-foot-tall clock tower in London. Of course, it tells Earth time, not Narnian time.

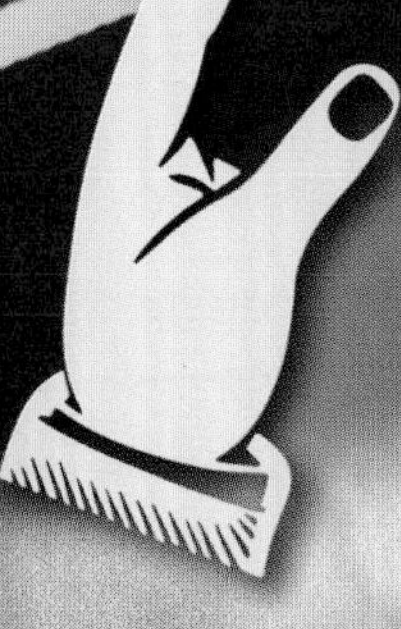

The cross of St. Patrick (diagonal red cross) is for Northern Ireland.

Country Living

Peter, Susan, Edmund and Lucy take the train from London to the country to stay with the Professor. The children find there isn't much to do on rainy days but explore the old house. Then they discover a wardrobe that's a passageway to another world—the magical land of Narnia!

It was the sort of house that you never seem to come to the end of, and it was full of unexpected places.

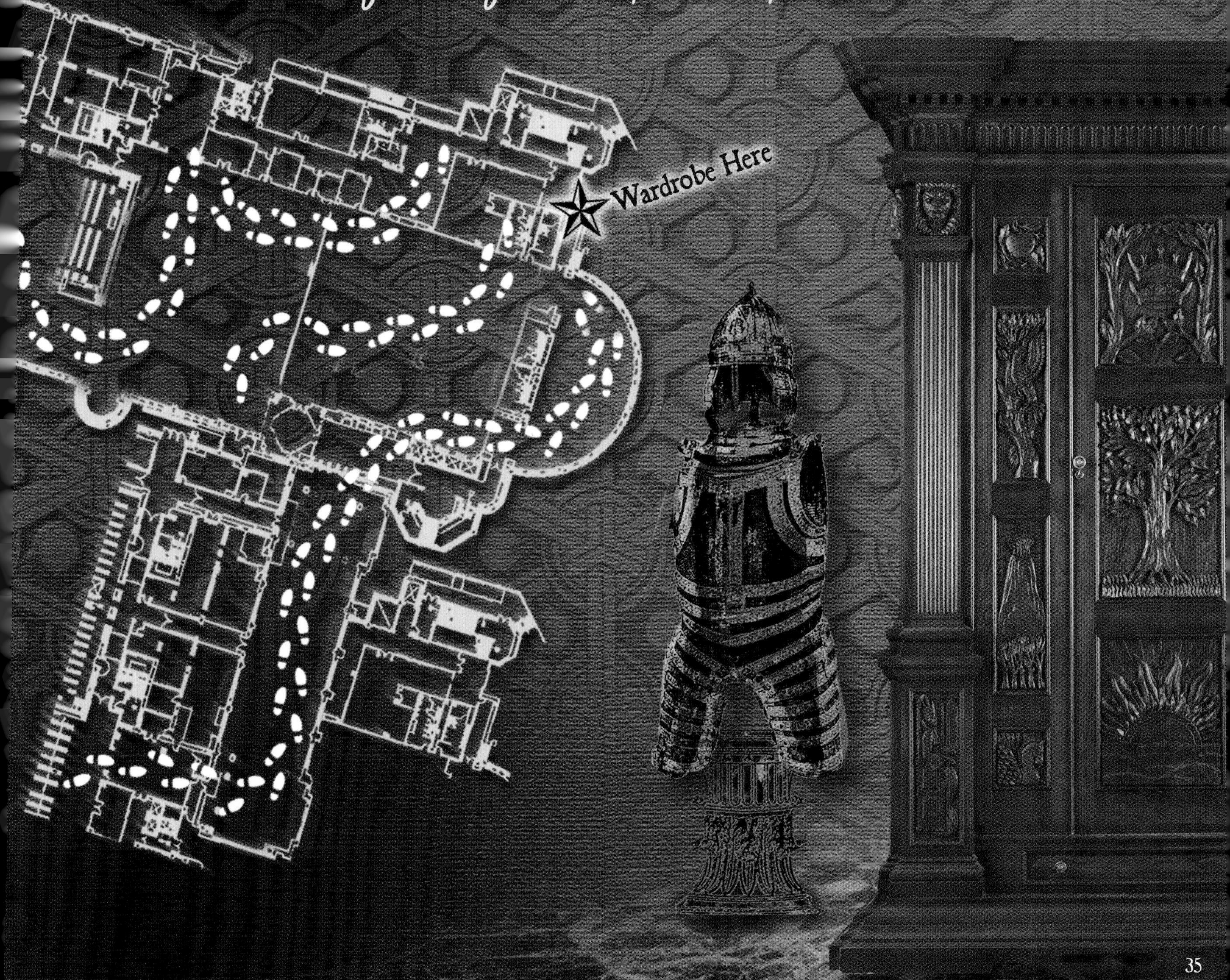

Wardrobe Here

Through the Wardrobe

While exploring the house the children discover a wardrobe in a spare room. Then, Lucy opens the door of the wardrobe. She steps inside, and instead of reaching the back of the wardrobe she lands in the snowy woods of Narnia.

The Wardrobe, Up Close and Personal

A wardrobe is a large wooden piece of furniture. It's like a closet for coats, clothes and blankets. (Lots of old houses don't have built-in closets.)

But this wardrobe is magical. Three times it becomes a door to Narnia:

- For Lucy alone
- For Lucy and Edmund
- For all four Pevensie children

TIME HERE, TIME THERE

Once you enter Narnia, no time passes in *our* world. The children spend years in Narnia as kings and queens, and yet when they travel back through the wardrobe and step into the spare room in the Professor's house, no time has passed.

Lucy finds a lamppost—standing right in the middle of a snowy wood! Here is where she meets Mr. Tumnus. The lamppost and the surrounding area, called Lantern Waste, mark the western end of Narnia.

Know More

How did the lamppost end up in the middle of the woods? By accident! The White Witch brought part of a London lamppost to Narnia to use as a weapon. After she threw it at Aslan, it dropped in the grass and grew into a lamppost.

HOMES, SWEET

WHAT HAPPENS THERE:

WHEN LUCY FIRST DISCOVERS NARNIA, SHE MEETS MR. TUMNUS AND GOES TO HIS CAVE HOUSE TO HAVE AFTERNOON TEA. SHE LEARNS ABOUT LIFE IN NARNIA AND THE WHITE WITCH. WHEN LUCY LATER RETURNS TO MR. TUMNUS'S HOUSE, SHE FINDS IT HAS BEEN RANSACKED BY THE WHITE WITCH'S SECRET POLICE AND MR. TUMNUS IS GONE.

Cozy Cave Available

- Fabulous wooded location; very private
- Clean, dry red-stone cave; 1 bedroom with fireplace
- Month-to-month rental (owner has been indefinitely detained)
- Completely furnished, including: carpet, two chairs, lamp, table, dresser, bookshelves

HOMES

Guests Welcome

- Friendly couple welcomes visitors to delightful dam
- Meals included
- Reasonable rates
- Great riverfront views!

WHAT HAPPENS THERE:

MR. BEAVER AND MRS. BEAVER FEED THE CHILDREN A LARGE MEAL AND TELL THEM ALL ABOUT NARNIA AND ASLAN.

HOME, BITTER HOME

The White Witch's Castle

CAUTION: RUINED CASTLE

The House was really a small castle. It seemed to be all towers; little towers with long pointed spires on them, sharp as needles. They looked like huge dunce's caps or sorcerer's caps. And they shone in the moonlight and their long shadows looked strange on the snow. Edmund began to be afraid of the House.

Abundant turrets, towers and spires (all extremely sharp and pointy)

More rooms than one can count

A bit musty and dusty

Iron gates and surrounding towers damaged

Large courtyard

Needs some work due to destruction by a giant

Solid

Previous

Big

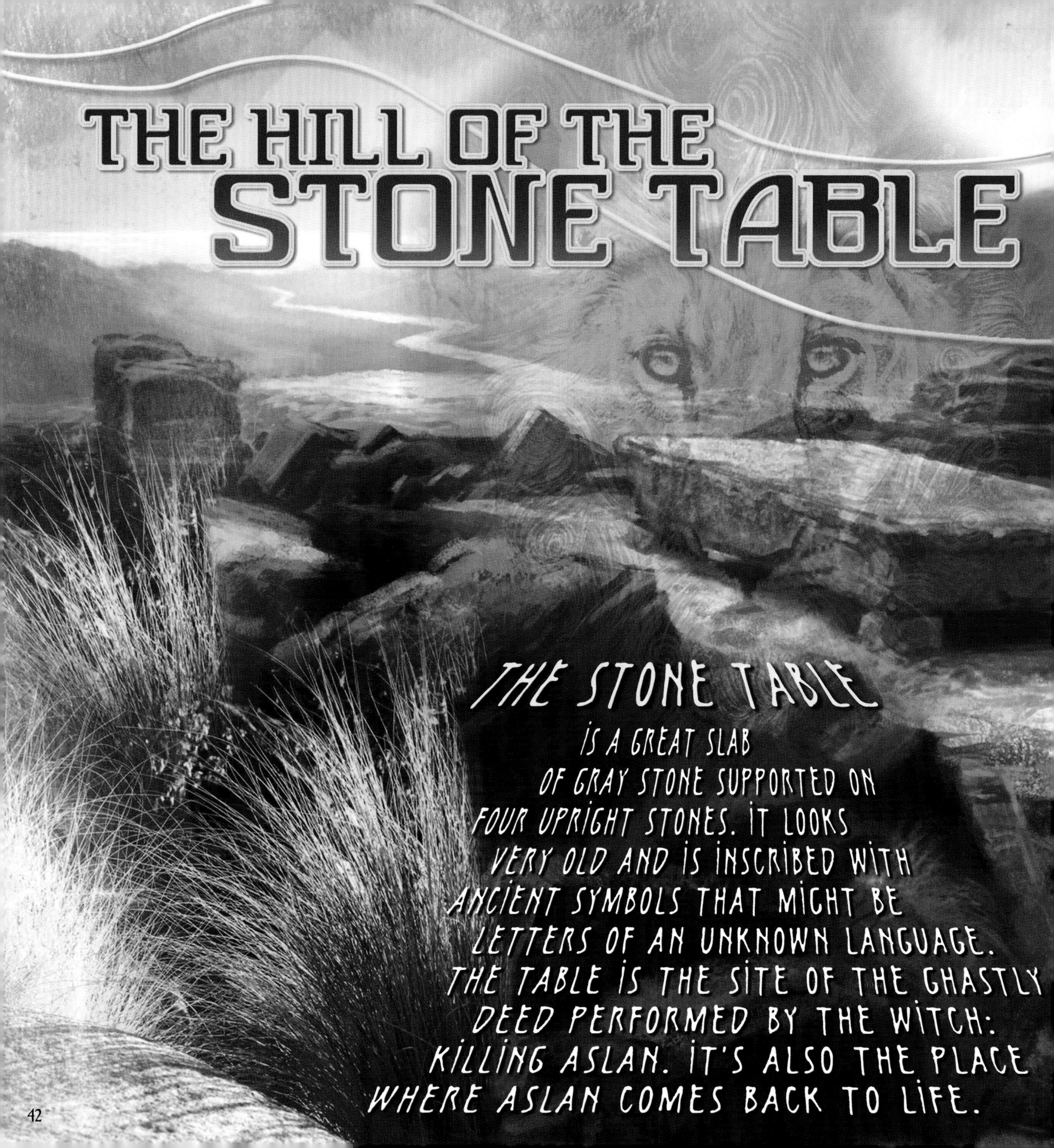

THE HILL OF THE STONE TABLE

THE STONE TABLE

is a great slab of gray stone supported on four upright stones. It looks very old and is inscribed with ancient symbols that might be letters of an unknown language. The table is the site of the ghastly deed performed by the Witch: killing Aslan. It's also the place where Aslan comes back to life.

From this open hilltop, you can see all the forests of Narnia, the Eastern Sea, and Cair Paravel.

THE CHILDREN FIRST MEET ASLAN NEAR THE STONE TABLE AT A PAVILION (A LARGE TENT) WITH A BANNER OF A RED LION FLYING ABOVE IT.

FIT FOR A KING (OR QUEEN)

Cair Paravel is the name of the castle that rests on a hill overlooking the Great River valley. Mr. Beaver recites an ancient Narnian poem that says when the four thrones of the castle are filled by humans, then the White Witch's reign will end. The rhyme goes like this:

When Adam's flesh and Adam's bone
Sits at Cair Paravel in throne,
The evil time will be over and done.

Castle tours every hour!

- Huge historic home fit for a king or queen
- Breathtaking ocean views from hilltop setting
- Spires and turrets galore
- Mermen and mermaids heard on occasion

"Once a king or queen in Narnia, always a king or queen."

PETER'S FIRST

Have you dreamed of being a hero?

MAYBE YOU IMAGINED CAPTURING A ROBBER OR SAVING SOMEONE FROM A BURNING BUILDING. AS PETER LEARNS, IMAGINING BRAVE FEATS AND DOING THEM ARE TWO DIFFERENT THINGS. AT FIRST, HE IS AN ORDINARY BOY, MUCH LIKE ANY OTHER 13 YEAR OLD. THEN HE GOES THROUGH THE WARDROBE.

PETER'S FIRST TEST OF COURAGE COMES WHEN THE WITCH SENDS MAUGRIM TO KILL THE CHILDREN. SUSAN BLOWS HER HORN; SHE NEEDS A HERO TO SAVE HER. ASLAN SAYS, "LET THE PRINCE WIN HIS SPURS." PETER DOES JUST THAT, KILLING MAUGRIM—ALTHOUGH HE IS SHAKY AND EXHAUSTED AFTER HE DOES IT.

Peter did not feel very brave; indeed, he felt he was going to be sick.

BATTLE

THE SWORD

POMMEL: "Cap" that helps hold the hilt together

EDGE: Sharp part of the blade, used for slashing

BLADE: Long sharp part

POINT: Very tip of the blade

HILT: Everything that is not the blade

QUILLON: Cross-piece of the sword, a type of guard

THE BATTLE WITH MAUGRIM IS THE FIRST TIME PETER NEEDS TO USE THE SWORD THAT FATHER CHRISTMAS GAVE HIM. SWORDS WERE FIRST MADE THOUSANDS OF YEARS AGO.

But that made no difference to what he had to do.

SAVED!

IN THE NICK OF TIME

Edmund misses Peter's heroics because the White Witch is about to cut his throat! But Aslan's army reaches Edmund in the nick of time.

He is saved!

WHEN THINGS AREN'T WHAT THEY SEEM

Animals and soldiers both protect themselves from their enemies by using camouflage (pronounced *CAM–oh–flahj*). They disguise themselves to blend in with their surroundings. A chameleon can change its skin color and pattern in less than a minute!

The Witch uses a special kind of camouflage because "it was part of her magic that she could make things look like what they aren't."

Things to Remember

- Never trust a strange lady with a wand who gives you candy.
- Never lie to your brother and sisters.
- Always keep up hope.

ALL IS NOT WON

When the quick battle is over, the Witch and her Dwarf can't be found. Where did they go? They are actually hiding in plain sight. The Witch disguises herself as a boulder and makes the Dwarf look like a tree stump.

THE BIG BATTLE

AFTER THE WITCH AGREES TO SPARE EDMUND'S LIFE, ASLAN TRIES TO PREPARE PETER FOR WHAT SHE WILL DO NEXT. AS THEY WALK TO THE FORDS OF BERUNA, THE LION AND PETER DISCUSS BATTLE PLANS. PETER IS SHOCKED WHEN ASLAN SAYS HE MIGHT MISS THE BATTLE. BUT, INDEED, ASLAN IS *NOT* PRESENT WHEN THE FINAL BATTLE AGAINST THE WITCH AND HER EVIL ARMY BEGINS.

THEN WITH A ROAR

How to Lead an Army

1. Recruit all types of soldiers. Giants and the Great Lion are especially helpful.

2. Identify your enemy's key weapons and destroy them.

3. Tend to all the wounded quickly.

THE TURNING POINT

Most wars have a key moment when the tide turns—when one side gains the upper hand. In the Big Battle, that moment belongs to Edmund when he smashes the Witch's wand to bits so that she can't turn any more of Peter's army into stone. Edmund is terribly wounded, but the tide is turned.

"Once her wand was broken we began to have some chance." —Peter

THAT SHOOK ALL NARNIA

FROM THE WESTERN LAMP-POST TO THE SHORES OF THE EASTERN SEA

THE GREAT BEAST FLUNG HIMSELF UPON THE WHITE WITCH.

Magic and

Magic is at the very heart of Narnia. Both good and evil creatures wield its power. In Narnia, there are three different levels of magic:

Magic: The White Witch uses magic to make enchanted Turkish Delight with her wand. The candy makes Edmund take her side, betraying his family and Aslan.

The Deep Magic:

According to the rules of the Deep Magic, the Witch owns the life of any betrayer. This is how the Witch claims the right to kill Edmund.

The Deeper Magic:

Aslan offers his own life in place of Edmund's. The Deeper Magic is strong enough to bring Aslan back to life.

mag·ic (MA-jik) *n.* 1. The practice of using charms, spells or rituals to attempt to produce supernatural effects or control events in nature. 2. The charms, spells and rituals so used.

Spells

Match these "Tools of the Trade" with the characters that *use* or *feel* their magic.

(Hint: Some have more than one correct answer.)

1. Turkish Delight:
Whoever eats it falls under the Witch's spell

2. Wand: Turns enemies to stone, makes enchanted Turkish Delight and does other terrible things

(Answers on last page)

3. The Wardrobe:
A doorway between Narnia and Earth

4. Horn:
Brings help from near and far

5. Cordial:
A liquid that heals the sick or injured

A White Witch
B Rumblebuffin
C Edmund
D Susan
E Lucy
F Peter
G Mr. Tumnus

The Deep Magic

The Deep Mag·ic (dEEp MA-jik)
n. 1. A special kind of magic the Emperor-beyond-the-Sea put into Narnia at the dawn of time. Under the law of the Deep Magic, every traitor belongs to the White Witch. 2. This is why the White Witch has a claim to kill Edmund.

The Deep Magic is **more powerful** than enchanted candy and magic wands. It has been around since the **beginning of Narnia**, and it **rules** how everyone must behave, including both the **good and the evil.** Its words are written in three special places—but most Narnians still don't completely understand it.

"Have you forgotten the Deep Magic?" asked the Witch. "Let us say I have forgotten it," answered Aslan gravely. "Tell us of this Deep Magic."

THE WORDS OF THE DEEP MAGIC APPEAR ON THE FIRE-STONES ON THE SECRET HILL IN LETTERS...

DEEP AS A SPEAR IS LONG

DEEPER THAN DEEP

The Deeper Magic is older and more powerful than the Deep Magic. The Witch thinks she has outsmarted Aslan: After she kills him, she thinks she can kill Edmund, too. But the Deep Magic only goes back to the dawn of time. Aslan knows the Deeper Magic, which says that when a willing person who has committed no crime is killed instead of a traitor, the Stone Table will crack and Death will start working backward. And so, thanks to the Deeper Magic, **ASLAN IS BORN AGAIN!**

"WHO'S DONE IT?" CRIED SUSAN.
"WHAT DOES IT MEAN? IS IT MORE MAGIC?"
"YES!" SAID A GREAT VOICE BEHIND THEIR BACKS.
"IT IS MORE MAGIC."

MAGIC IN ACTION

MAGIC POWERS, LIKE SCIENCE, CAN BE USED TO DO EVIL OR GOOD. THESE CREATURES OF NARNIA FEEL THE EFFECTS OF BOTH...

...AS THEY ARE TURNED INTO STONE STATUES BY THE WITCH...

WITCH'S MAGIC WAND

...AND THEN LIBERATED BY ASLAN'S LIFE-GIVING BREATH.

EVERYWHERE THE STATUES WERE COMING TO LIFE. THE COURTYARD LOOKED NO LONGER LIKE A MUSEUM; IT LOOKED MORE LIKE A ZOO.

The Magic Continues

Lucy is the first to peer into the wardrobe and step out in the snowy Lantern Waste of Narnia.

THE LION, THE WITCH AND THE WARDROBE is not the end of the story of Narnia—or the beginning either! It happens to be the first book that C. S. Lewis wrote to tell the whole story of Narnia. It is also the first of the seven books in THE CHRONICLES OF NARNIA to be made into a movie. The movie makers at Walt Disney Pictures and Walden Media have joined forces to bring the magic and adventure of Narnia to life. The movie lets you see THE LION, THE WITCH AND THE WARDROBE on the screen. The other six books of Narnia stories let you see the rest of the great tale.

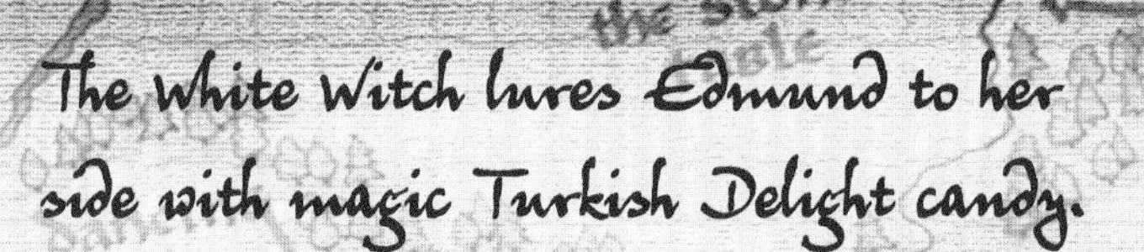

The White Witch lures Edmund to her side with magic Turkish Delight candy.

Father Christmas has gifts for the children. Peter gets a sword and a shield with Aslan's red symbol on it.

Susan, Peter and Lucy bravely fight many battles to rescue Narnia from the Witch's evil magic.

...AND CONTINUES

The Witch is furious and frightened as the tide of the great battle turns against her.

Lucy watches as Susan practices with her bow to prepare for battle against the Witch.

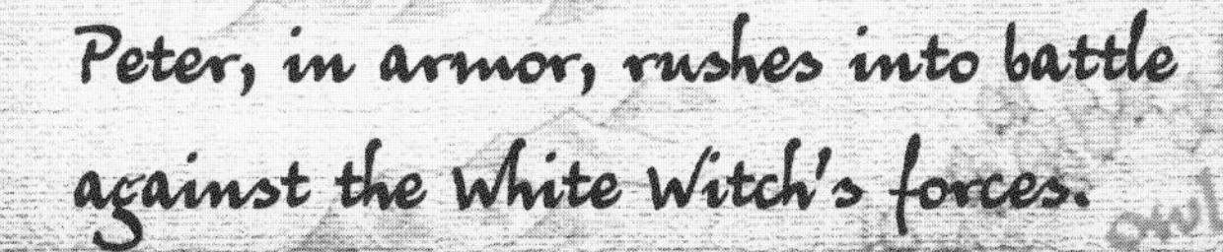

Peter, in armor, rushes into battle against the White Witch's forces.

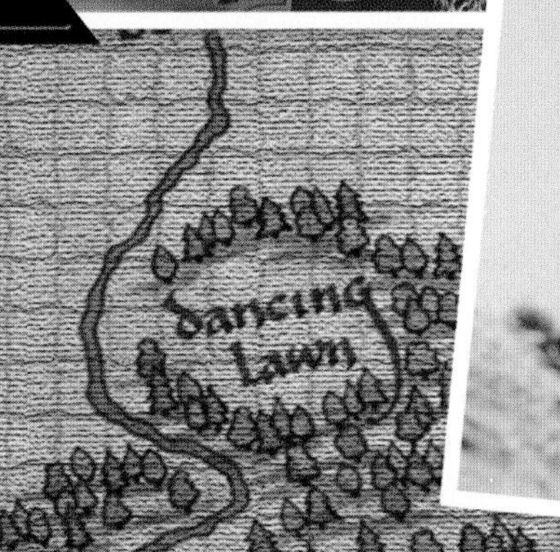

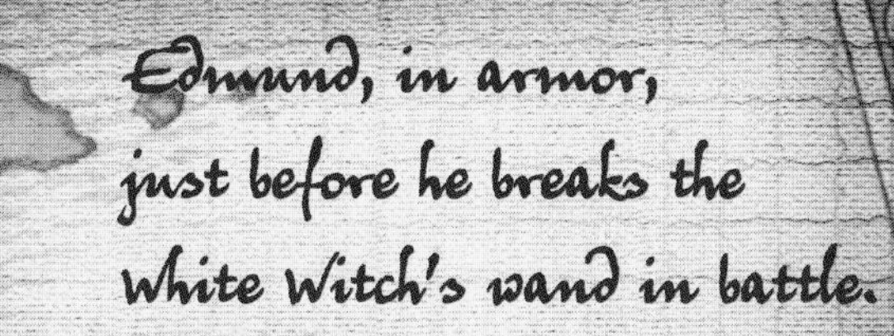

Edmund, in armor, just before he breaks the White Witch's wand in battle.

After the Witch's defeat, Peter, Lucy, Susan and Edmund are crowned High Kings and High Queens of Narnia at Cair Paravel.

ANSWERS

SUSAN: CAN YOU HEAR ME? C

PETER: OTHER FAMOUS LEADERS MATCH: 1. C; 2. B; 3. A; 4. E; 5. F; 6. D

ASLAN'S MAGICAL MOMENT: Some small creatures who made a big difference: David and Goliath, Dorothy from *The Wizard of Oz*, Jack and the Beanstalk and Stuart Little.

MAGIC AND SPELLS: TOOLS OF THE TRADE MATCH: 1. A, C; 2. A, B, C, G; 3. C, D, E, F; 4. D, F; 5. C, E

The story continues in the six other books of *The Chronicles of Narnia*: *The Magician's Nephew*, *The Horse and His Boy*, *Prince Caspian*, *The Voyage of the* Dawn Treader, *The Silver Chair*, *The Last Battle*.

Credits

Editorial consulting by Douglas Gresham, co-producer of the movie *The Chronicles of Narnia: The Lion, the Witch and the Wardrobe* and authority on C. S. Lewis and his works.

This book was created by jacob packaged goods LLC using computer illustration and composition to combine art, photography and type. Creative for jacob packaged goods (www.jpgglobal.com): Ellen Jacob, Dawn Camner, Cathrine Wolf, Susan Brody, Jenny McGuirk, Kirk Cheyfitz

All art by Disney Enterprises, Inc. and Walden Media, LLC, used by permission. All art by Pauline Baynes, used by permission of C.S. Lewis Pte. Ltd. All art by Tudor Humphries, used by permission of C.S. Lewis Pte. Ltd. All art by Cliff Nielsen, used by permission of C.S. Lewis Pte. Ltd. *Half-title, copyright, and title:* Disney Enterprises, Inc. and Walden Media, LLC. *Contents:* Backgrounds: Disney Enterprises, Inc. and Walden Media, LLC. *This Side of the Wardrobe:* Professor's house: Disney Enterprises, Inc. and Walden Media, LLC; Wardrobe and Lucy entering wardrobe: Pauline Baynes. *The White Witch's Winter:* Background: Disney Enterprises, Inc. and Walden Media, LLC; Lamppost and Lucy with Mr. Tumnus: Pauline Baynes; Mr. and Mrs. Beaver and the Witch's castle: Disney Enterprises, Inc. and Walden Media, LLC; The Witch's sledge and Edmund: Tudor Humphries. *The Age of Aslan:* Background: Disney Enterprises, Inc. and Walden Media, LLC; Aslan, Father Christmas and the Stone Table: Tudor Humphries; Cair Paravel and the battle: Pauline Baynes. *Lucy:* Lucy portrait and Father Christmas: Tudor Humphries; Dagger: Disney Enterprises, Inc. and Walden Media, LLC. *Edmund:* Aslan and Edmund's back: Disney Enterprises, Inc. and Walden Media, LLC; Edmund: Tudor Humphries. *Susan:* Susan portrait: Tudor Humphries; Quiver, horn, arrows and sword: Disney Enterprises, Inc. and Walden Media, LLC. *Peter:* Background, sword and shield: Disney Enterprises, Inc. and Walden Media, LLC; Peter and Father Christmas: Tudor Humphries; Battle and Cair Paravel: Pauline Baynes. *Riding the Lion:* Background, Mr. Beaver and black dwarf: Disney Enterprises, Inc. and Walden Media, LLC. *Aslan's Most Magical Moment:* Background and filmstrip images: Disney Enterprises, Inc. and Walden Media, LLC. *Friends and Helpers:* Mr. and Mrs. Beaver, Mr. Tumnus and Father Christmas: Tudor Humphries. *Wanted: White Witch:* The White Witch and Aslan: Tudor Humphries. *Evil Creatures:* Background and black dwarf: Disney Enterprises, Inc. and Walden Media, LLC; Maugrim: Tudor Humphries. *Horrible Henchmen:* Boggle, Minotaur, Werewolf, Ogre and Specter: Disney Enterprises, Inc. and Walden Media, LLC. *Cheerio!:* Pevensie Children: Pauline Baynes; Professor's House: Disney Enterprises, Inc. and Walden Media, LLC. *Country Living:* Forest background, Professor's house and wardrobe: Disney Enterprises, Inc. and Walden Media, LLC. *Through the Wardrobe:* Background: Disney Enterprises, Inc. and Walden Media, LLC; Wardrobe, Lucy exiting wardrobe and lamppost: Tudor Humphries. *Homes, Sweet Homes:* Mr. Tumnus's house and The Beavers' house: Disney Enterprises, Inc. and Walden Media, LLC. *Home, Bitter Home:* Background, castle inset left and castle far right: Disney Enterprises, Inc. and Walden Media, LLC; The White Witch, castle background and castle courtyard: Tudor Humphries. *The Hill of the Stone Table:* Stone Table background: Disney Enterprises, Inc. and Walden Media, LLC; Aslan: Cliff Nielsen. *Fit for a King (or Queen):* Background, Mr. Beaver and Cair Paravel: Disney Enterprises, Inc. and Walden Media, LLC; Pevensie children on throne: Pauline Baynes. *Peter's First Battle:* Peter and Maugrim: Tudor Humphries; Shield and sword: Disney Enterprises, Inc. and Walden Media, LLC. *Saved! In the Nick of Time:* Background and black dwarf: Disney Enterprises, Inc. and Walden Media, LLC; Aslan, Edmund and the White Witch: Tudor Humphries. *The Big Battle:* Battle scene, shield and axe: Disney Enterprises, Inc. and Walden Media, LLC; Edmund inset: Tudor Humphries. *Magic and Spells:* Cordial bottle: Disney Enterprises, Inc. and Walden Media, LLC; Wardrobe: Pauline Baynes. *The Deep Magic:* Background, Stone Table and cherry dryad: Disney Enterprises, Inc. and Walden Media, LLC; The White Witch and Aslan: Tudor Humphries. *Deeper Than Deep:* Background and Stone Table: Disney Enterprises, Inc. and Walden Media, LLC; Aslan leaping: Pauline Baynes. *Magic in Action:* Background, Mr. Tumnus and centaur: Disney Enterprises, Inc. and Walden Media, LLC; Aslan: Cliff Nielsen. *The Magic Continues . . . And Continues:* Background and photos: Disney Enterprises, Inc. and Walden Media, LLC. *Answers and Credits:* Background: Disney Enterprises, Inc. and Walden Media, LLC.